SANDI and the Ladybug

Written by Sandi Towers-Romero
Illustrated by Teresa Abboud

BASED ON A TRUE STORY!

PROLANCE

Prolance

www.prolancewriting.com
California, USA
©2019 Sandi Towers-Romero
Illustrations ©2019 Teresa Abboud

ISBN: 978-0-9996991-5-7

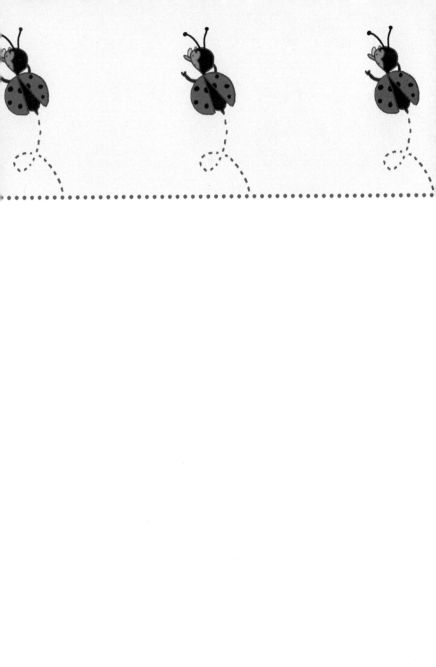

"Tonight, can you help me fix our salad?" asked Sandi's father.

"Sure Dad, what should I do?"

She loved helping her father fix dinner.

"Please take off the wilted leaves from the romaine lettuce."

She took the lettuce, and sat next to the trash basket. She took off one leaf, then another, and then to her surprise she found a beautiful red, with black spots, *ladybug*!

"Hi!" Sandi said to the ladybug. "What's your name? My name is Sandi."

"My name is Walter, nice meeting you," said the ladybug.

"Walter! That is a funny name for a ladybug."

"There are boy ladybugs," Walter said, giggling.

"Oh!" Sandi giggled too, and said, "I've never thought about that."

"What are you doing in the lettuce?" Sandi asked.

"I was hired, by Farmer Brown, to help him take care of the lettuce."

"Hired?" Sandi asked.

"Yes, I work for him."

"Who is Farmer Brown?"
Sandi asked.

"He is the farmer that
grows your lettuce."

"Where is his farm?" Sandi asked.

"I don't know," Walter said. "But, can you get me back to the farm?"

"I will try," replied Sandi.

"Dad, can I use the computer?" Sandi asked.

"Yes, as long as you are not too long, dinner is almost ready."

So, Sandi put Walter on her shoulder and walked over to the family laptop. She typed in, F-A-R-M-E-R B-R-O-W-N.

Some websites came up. Walter grew excited, but then saddened when these were for a restaurant.

Sandi added Romaine lettuce to her search. Sandi and Walter grew excited again, but Walter moaned when no matches to the search appeared.

"I know, I will ask my father for help," she said.

"Dad, could you help us? I found Walter, the ladybug, in the lettuce. He works for Farmer Brown, and wants to go home."

Sandi's father was shocked to see a ladybug sitting on her shoulder. He told her he would be happy to help. Sandi's father went Online and did find a phone number for a Farmer Brown.

Sandi and Walter grew excited again. But, when her father called, the Farmer Brown he found did not grow lettuce, only pumpkins.

Walter heard this and was sad.

Sandi was sad too, but had a great idea.

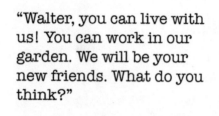

"Walter, you can live with us! You can work in our garden. We will be your new friends. What do you think?"

Walter thought about this offer. Sandi was nervous, she wanted her new friend to stay.

After, what seemed like forever, Walter said, "Yes, I would like that."

Sandi jumped for joy!

So every morning, Sandi would let Walter out.

He would fly to the garden, and stay all day.

Each evening, Walter would come back to their kitchen window and Sandi would let him in.

Walter was happy. Sandi was happy, and Sandi's father was happy too!

Author:

Teaching is Sandi's greatest passion. At the age of seventeen, she received her Water Safety Instructor's certification, and since then, she has taught hundreds of children to swim and feel comfortable in the water.

While a student at Arizona State University, she taught 5th and 6th grade math and science. After receiving her Juris Doctor's degree, from Western State University College of Law, she was the editor for the publication, "Speaking of Legal Aid." This publication, a product of Orange County, California's Legal Aid Society, was dedicated to explaining the law to non-lawyers.

She now teaches law, and college success classes, at Florida South Western State College, in Fort Myers, Florida. She has also taught law at Florida Southern College, South Florida Community College; and has lectured, on the law, at University of California, Irvine. She has three law textbooks: Essentials of Florida Real Estate Law; Media and Entertainment Law, and Law and the Hospitality Industry.

While living in Hawaii, she published three magazines; dedicated to educating the business community of Hawaii, and imparting Hawaiian cultural information to Hawaii visitors. She has received Small Business Association awards for Media Advocate and Women in Business Advocate, for the County of Hawaii.

Illustrator:
Teresa Abboud is a Georgia-based illustrator and a
2D animator. She graduated from the Académie
Libanaise des Beaux Arts. She grew up in Lebanon
in an artistic environment, in an atmosphere of
integrity and disorder, war and liberty. Teresa's
art reflects her inner feelings. Her aesthetic choices
come directly from this atmosphere that marked her
childhood. Teresa wants to tell stories, share feelings,
express ideas, and transmit emotions through her art.
www.teresaafternoon.com

In this, Sandi's first children's book, she hopes to teach our youngest generation that all creatures big or, even as small as a ladybug, should be honored and cherished.